Allie THE ALLERGIC ELEPHANT

by Nicole Smith

illustrated by Maggie Nichols

May every peanut-allergic child learn to say "No, thank you,"
and yet enjoy being part of a group of friends.

Nicole Smith

Allie THE ALLERGIC ELEPHANT

A Children's Story of Peanut Allergies

Publisher's Cataloging-in-Publication

Smith, Nicole S.
    Allie the allergic elephant : [a children's story of peanut allergies] / by Nicole Smith ; illustrated by Maggie Nichols. -- 3rd ed.
    22 p. .3 cm.
    SUMMARY: Allie the elephant has an allergic reaction to peanuts served at school, and soon learns what symptoms to watch for and what foods to avoid.
    Audience: Preschool–1st grade.
    ISBN: 978-1-58628-053-6
    ISBN: 1-58628-053-8

    1. Food allergy--Juvenile fiction. 2. Peanuts--Juvenile fiction. 3. Elephants--Juvenile fiction.
4. Allergens--Juvenile fiction. [1. Food allergy--Fiction.
2. Peanuts--Fiction. 3. Elephants--Fiction.]
I. Nichols, Maggie (Maggie Alison) II. Title

PZ7.S6567A1 2006   [E]

ISBN: 978-1-58628-053-6
ISBN: 1-58628-053-8

Text © Copyright 2002, 2004, 2006 by Allergic Child Publishing Group
Illustrations © Copyright 2002, 2004, 2006 by
Allergic Child Publishing Group

Printed in Mexico

For more information regarding permissions or how to get additional copies, contact the publisher:

Allergic Child Publishing Group
425 W. Rockrimmon Blvd, Suite 202
Colorado Springs, CO 80919

www.allergicchild.com

Allergic Child

Dealing with Severe Food Allergies

Thank you, Morgan, for the inspiration. — N.S.

Allie is a special elephant. She is loved by her mother, her father,
her brother and her friends.

Allie loves to go to school and to eat.

Elephants love to eat peanuts.

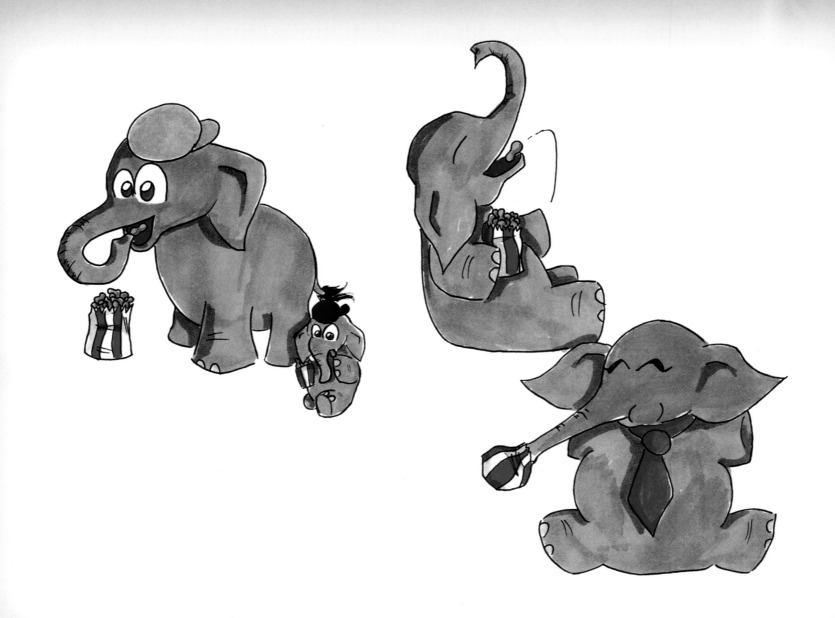

Allie would love to eat peanuts like other elephants.
But peanuts don't like Allie.

Peanuts make Allie itch... and swell... and feel terrible!
That means Allie is allergic to peanuts.

Allie even wears a special bracelet to tell people she's allergic to peanuts. Allie's parents also carry an epinephrine kit in case Allie accidentally eats peanuts.

Sometimes Allie wishes she could eat peanuts like the other animals at school.

Some of Allie's friends feel bad for her. They want to share
their peanuts with Allie so she won't feel left out.

What do you think would happen to Allie
if her friends gave her peanuts?

Oh no... Allie is having hives from the peanuts!
Do you want to see Allie get hives?

Oh no... Allie is having swelled lips from the peanuts!
Do you want to see Allie get swelled lips?

Oh no... Allie is having red eyes from the peanuts!
Do you want to see Allie have red eyes?

Oh no... Allie is having an itchy nose from the peanuts!
Do you want to see Allie having an itchy nose?

Oh no... Allie is coughing from the peanuts!
Do you want to see Allie coughing?

Or would you rather see Allie stay healthy and happy?

Allie wants to stay healthy and she knows to say "No, thank you"
to the peanuts her friends offer her.

Allie likes to eat snacks like carrots or bananas.

Allie always asks if there's a peanut hidden someplace in the food that a friend gives her. Do you know which foods peanuts hide in?

Peanut butter, chocolate candy bars, ice cream, Chinese food, and even plain M&M's® all hide peanuts!

Allie has learned to stay away from foods that have peanuts in them.
And she still has plenty of foods to choose from!

Allie just wants to be a normal elephant that loves to
go to school, loves her family and loves to eat.

She just gets to eat food other than peanuts.
And that makes Allie very special!

A Note to Parents

This book was written to help my preschool aged son and his classmates understand his peanut allergy. The foods mentioned here are but a partial list of foods that "hide" peanuts. I'm sure that you carefully read labels as we do. Peanuts show up in the most unsuspected foods!

I hope this book will help your child and friends understand peanut allergies in a fun, loving way—even though the allergy can be life threatening.

More specific information regarding peanut allergies is available at: www.allergicchild.com

A Note to Teachers

There are different levels of peanut allergies. Some children are so allergic that inhaling the peanut dust will give them a life threatening reaction. Other children react by getting hives upon touching peanuts, also known as a contact reaction. Still others will have a reaction only upon ingesting a peanut or peanut product.

The severity of the reaction will dictate what accommodations need to be made in the classroom and in the school. It is sometimes difficult to be careful enough.

We have found the best results occur when the parents, teacher, school nurse and child together formulate a plan. The most important ingredient is information.

When the child feels supported, no longer is there fear.

An epinephrine kit will most likely accompany the child to school if the child's physician feels there is a risk for anaphylaxis. We've found it is important for everyone involved to have training on the specifics of administering this kit before being faced with the need to use it!

More specific information regarding peanut allergies is available at: www.allergicchild.com.

More Information

Visit our Web site at:
www.allergicchild.com

- Food Allergy Book & Magazine Recommendations are listed for children's books, cookbooks and parenting the food allergic child.

- Specific information about allergies, allergic reactions and anaphylaxis is provided in a readable, understandable format for parents of newly diagnosed children.

- Allergy support group listings for every state in the USA, plus across Europe and beyond.

- Listing of safe restaurants and safe play places across the USA for the food allergic child and their family.

- Classroom signs featuring No Peanuts and No Nuts are available for purchase:

Digital e-books are available:

- "Sending Your Food Allergic Child to School"

- "Food Allergic Children and Schools: Support for Teachers & Administrators"

- "Traveling and Eating Out with Food Allergies"

- "How to Help Your Child Succeed with Food Allergy & Behavior Manifestations: Giftedness, Autism & Attention Deficit Hyperactivity Disorder"

Allergic *Child*
Dealing with Severe Food Allergies

M&M's® is a registered trademark of Mars, Incorporated

Other Sources of Information

There are other organizations and Web sites that have an abundance of information on the topic of peanut allergies and other food allergies:

Kids With Food Allergies
www.kidswithfoodallergies.org

Peanutallergy.com
www.peanutallergy.com

Food Allergy Initiative
www.foodallergyinitiative.org

The Food Allergy & Anaphylaxis Network (FAAN)
www.foodallergy.org